DUNCAN

Based on *The Railway Series* by the Rev. W. Awdry

Illustrations by
Robin Davies and Jerry Smith

EGMONT

EGMONT

We bring stories to life

First published in Great Britain in 2004
by Egmont UK Limited
239 Kensington High Street, London W8 6SA
This edition published in 2008
All Rights Reserved

HiT entertainment

ISBN 978 1 4052 3464 1

1 3 5 7 9 10 8 6 4 2

Printed in Italy

The Forest Stewardship Council (FSC) is an international, non-governmental organisation
dedicated to promoting responsible management of the world's forests. FSC operates a
system of forest certification and product labelling that allows consumers to identify
wood and wood-based products from well managed forests.

For more information about Egmont's paper buying policy please visit www.egmont.co.uk/ethicalpublishing

For more information about the FSC please visit their website at www.fsc.uk.org

This is a story about Duncan the Narrow-Gauge Engine. Duncan used to complain about his passengers. But this changed when Skarloey told a story about how Rheneas saved the Railway . . .

One morning, Skarloey was in the Yard, being polished by Nancy, the Guard's daughter.

Skarloey was thinking about his friend Rheneas, who had gone away to be mended.

"Rheneas comes home tomorrow," said Nancy.

"What? Tomorrow?" chirped Skarloey. "I must look my very best! Please polish me some more!"

"You're such an old fuss pot!" laughed Nancy.

Duncan was jealous. "Aren't you going to polish me, too?" he asked.

"Sorry, I have to get the ice lollies ready for the passengers," said Nancy.

"It's not fair," Duncan complained. "Peter Sam gets a new funnel, Sir Handel gets special wheels, passengers get ice lollies, but I'm not even polished!"

Duncan enjoyed complaining and he soon began to sulk.

That afternoon, there was bad news from up the line.

"One of Skarloey's coaches has derailed," called Duncan's Driver. "We'll have to go there right away."

Duncan took the workmen to sort out the mess. "All this extra work!" he grumbled. "It wears an engine out."

The derailed coach was in the middle of the train, so Skarloey had gone on to the Top Station with the front coaches.

Duncan brought the rear coaches home. He sulked all the way back to the station. "I get no rest! I get no rest!" he muttered.

He arrived back just in time for his own 4 o'clock train. But he was sulky and wouldn't move.

"Come on, we're keeping our passengers waiting," his Driver reminded him.

At last they set off.

Shortly before the next station, they came to a viaduct and Duncan ground to a halt.

"I've had enough. I'm staying here!" he snapped.

And he did, too!

Skarloey had to come down from the Top Station to haul Duncan and his train to the platform.

The passengers were furious. They burst out of the train and told the Drivers, the Firemen and the Guard what a bad Railway it was.

Duncan was still sulky. "Why should I have to work hard, just to pull silly old passengers?" he asked.

But no one was listening to him.

The Thin Controller was waiting for Duncan at the Shed.

"If you won't carry passengers, you won't get polished," he said, sternly.

"I'd rather not be polished if it meant I didn't have to carry passengers," Duncan muttered to himself. But he didn't dare say it loud enough for The Thin Controller to hear!

"I'm ashamed of you, Duncan!" said Skarloey that night. "You should think of your passengers, not yourself."

"Passengers are just nuisances. They're always complaining," replied Duncan.

"That's no way to talk!" said Skarloey. "We need passengers. No passengers means no trains. And no trains means no Railway! I remember when Rheneas saved our Railway because he cared about the passengers."

"Please tell us about it!" said Peter Sam.

Skarloey began: "Rheneas knew we had to keep the trains running or our Railway would have to close. He was often short of steam, but he always struggled on to a station and then rested when he got there.

'I mustn't stop between stations,' he'd say. 'The passengers wouldn't like it.'"

"Pshaw!" huffed Duncan. He had stopped on a viaduct and hadn't cared at all.

"One wet and windy afternoon," Skarloey continued, "when the rails were damp, Rheneas was travelling home with a full train.

'Aaah! I've got cramp!' he groaned, suddenly. And he stopped on the loneliest part of the line.

His Driver examined him. 'Your valve gear has jammed. We need to reach the next station. Do you think you can get us there?' he asked.

'I'll try,' replied Rheneas, bravely.

"So The Thin Controller sanded the rails, some passengers pushed from behind, and Rheneas jerked and began to move forward.

'I'll get there or burst! I'll get there or burst!' Rheneas muttered to himself. And he moved slowly along the track until he finally reached the station.

'Thank you for getting us home,' the passengers said. 'We'll tell all our friends that this is a really fine Railway!' "

"And so you see what a brave engine Rheneas is," said Skarloey to Duncan.

"Thank you for telling us about him," whispered Duncan. "I was wrong. Passengers are important after all!"

The next day, Rheneas came home. The engines greeted him with a chorus of whistles.

But the loudest whistle came from Duncan, who decided he would always put passengers first from then on!

The Thomas Story Library is THE definitive collection of stories about Thomas and ALL his friends.

5 more Thomas Story Library titles will be chuffing into your local bookshop in August 2008!

Jeremy

Hector

BoCo

Billy

Whiff

And there are even more Thomas Story Library books to follow late

So go on, start your Thomas Story Library NOW!

A Fantastic Offer for Thomas the Tank Engine Fans!

In every Thomas Story Library book like this one, you will find a special token. Collect 6 Thomas tokens and we will send you a brilliant Thomas poster, and a double-sided bedroom door hanger! Simply tape a £1 coin in the space above, and fill out the form overleaf.

TO BE COMPLETED BY AN ADULT

To apply for this great offer, ask an adult to complete the coupon below
and send it with a pound coin and 6 tokens, to:
THOMAS OFFERS, PO BOX 715, HORSHAM RH12 5WG

☐ Please send a Thomas poster and door hanger. I enclose 6 tokens
plus a £1 coin. (Price includes P&P)

Fan's name...

Address...

....Postcode...............................

Date of birth...

Name of parent/guardian..

Signature of parent/guardian...